W9-AQI-138

# Lightning Inside You

·

## and Other Native American Riddles

·

·

*William Morrow & Company*

·

NEW YORK

# Lightning Inside You

and Other

Native American

Riddles

·

Edited by John Bierhorst

·

*Illustrated by Louise Brierley*

FRANKLIN PIERCE
COLLEGE LIBRARY
RINDGE, N.H. 03461

Text copyright © 1992 by John Bierhorst
Illustrations copyright © 1992 by Louise Brierley

All rights reserved.
No part of this book may be reproduced
or utilized in any form or by any means, electronic or mechanical,
including photocopying, recording or by any information storage
and retrieval system, without permission in writing from the Publisher.
Inquiries should be addressed to
William Morrow and Company, Inc.,
1350 Avenue of the Americas, New York, N.Y. 10019.

Printed in the United States of America.
Designed by Jane Byers Bierhorst
2   4   6   8   10   9   7   5   3   1

Library of Congress Cataloging-in-Publication Data

Lightning inside you : riddles of the American Indians
edited by John Bierhorst
illustrations by Louise Brierley.
p.   cm.
Includes bibliographical references.
ISBN 0-688-09582-8
1. Riddles, Indian.   2. Indians—Humor.   3. Indians—Folklore.
PN6377.I48L54      1992      398.6'0897-dc20      91-21744      CIP

*Acknowledgment is made to publishers and other copyright
holders for permission to quote or translate
riddles appearing in this book. For specific acknowledgments
see the section entitled "Who the Riddlers Are," and compare
"Sources" for full bibliographic information.*

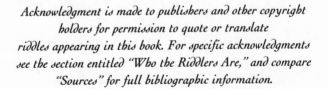

# *Foreword*

There have been many riddle books, but this is the first to gather up the riddles of Native America.

Fifty years ago, it was widely believed that there were no American Indian riddles. And as recently as twenty years ago, some people were still wondering whether there were or weren't.

The reason for doubt was that some of the older sources were poorly known and some of the newer ones had not yet been made available. So few Indian riddles were in circulation that scholars tended to think they had been borrowed from Europeans.

Riddling, like fever, is contagious. And it is true that some Indian riddles (including some in this book) have been borrowed from the Old World. Perhaps the present collection will stimulate borrowing in the other direction. Surely it will help put an end to the mistaken idea that riddling does not belong to the western hemisphere.

A number of individuals and institutions have assisted me in my search for Native American riddles. In particular, I would like to thank Richard Dauenhauer; David Guss; Anatilde Idoyaga Molina; Frank Salomon; and the staff of the Alaska Native Language Center, Fairbanks, Alaska.

J.B.

*West Shokan, N.Y.*

# Contents

# Native Riddling
# in the Americas

"When folks riddle, all things are people to them." So explains Chief Henry — an elder of the Koyukon tribe of central Alaska — revealing one of the most important tricks for solving American Indian riddles.

In other words, the riddle itself may seem to talk about a person. But the answer is actually a thing or an animal.

This is true of many of the riddles known to Chief Henry's tribe and of countless riddles told by Native people in other parts of North, South, and Central America. As it happens, half the riddles in this book are "people" riddles that are really about things or animals.

Among the Alaskan Koyukon, the "folks," or villagers, that Chief Henry had in mind used to get together during the late winter and use riddles to pass the time. It was even said that this helped to make the long Alaskan nights grow shorter. If someone came up with an answer that made sense, though it was not the answer the riddler was thinking of, the riddler would say, "*haku*," meaning "very good," or "almost right."

This must have been welcome encouragement, because some Indian riddles, in spite of tricks for solving them, can be difficult. In fact, there are reports of riddling sessions that have gone on for hours or even days, stuck on a single riddle.

Hard ones are included in this book. Yet many are not impossible to guess, and some are surprisingly easy.

As an experiment, I recently tried out a few of these

riddles on two kinds of audiences. First, on groups of adults gathered at the University of Oklahoma and at the American Museum of Natural History in New York City. Second, on groups of fourth graders and sixth graders at a public school in upstate New York.

The adults did fairly well. But the grade-school audiences did even better, showing more persistence and more creativity. Here are some of the younger groups' answers to the old Maya riddle "I am doing it, and you are doing it. Can you guess what it is?"

sitting
thinking
talking
listening
hearing
watching
staring
breathing

Each of these answers deserves an appreciative *"haku."* And the last, "breathing," is the Native answer.

Here is a harder one: "What is it that never gets tired of motioning people to come over?" The grade-schoolers offered these guesses:

your friends
people
the police
teachers
your parents
leaders
missionaries who came to the Indians

Again, each answer deserves a *"haku"* (especially the last, which shows that the guesser knew something about Indian history). However, this is an example of a "people" riddle that is not actually about people. The Native answer is "the earflaps of the tepee."

(I have now given away two of the riddles in this book. But in fact, the ability to remember answers to riddles that one has heard before is another important "trick" in riddling. Remembering is not cheating.)

As I have mentioned, the younger audiences in my experiment were quicker with answers. Perhaps equally important, they were less willing to see the humor in Indian riddles. By contrast, the museum and university audiences found some of the answers amusing and filled the room with laughter when they heard them.

Of the adults who attempted to give their own answers, most made it obvious that they considered riddling a game. This was less clear with the grade-schoolers, who were quite serious, never laughing out loud.

Both attitudes are correct, and both are present in Indian tradition.

In the old days, some kinds of riddles were used in life-or-death situations or as part of an important ritual. There was nothing amusing about them. In other cases, as with the Koyukon of Alaska, riddles were frankly a pastime, a form of entertainment; this was equally true among the Penobscot of Maine, where village "riddle-men" would stop people on the road and quiz them. In still other cases, riddling was part ritual and part pastime, to be taken seriously but also to be enjoyed.

A look at some of the different riddling situations will show the variety and richness of this Native American tradition.

## Hunters' riddles

Out of either respect or fear, hunters used to avoid calling game animals by their actual names. For example, in many Canadian tribes a black bear or a grizzly bear would be called "Grandfather," "Friend," "Black Food," "Short Tail," or "Supernatural One." In extreme cases, the manner of speaking could take the form of a riddle.

Among the Sirionó, a tribe of Bolivia, a woman meeting her husband, who had just come back from hunting, might say to him, "Did you kill nothing?" The husband, who had killed game but had not yet carried it home, might then say, "Slimy palm seed."

In this way the wife would know that her husband had killed a deer — because when deer eat palm fruits, they leave the seeds slimy.

A similar custom was observed by the Kutchin tribe of Alaska, whose men told riddles to let each other know that a bear's den had been sighted. If a man found a place where a bear was living, he would have to go for help, because it would be too dangerous for one hunter alone to try to make the kill.

The man might go to his neighbor and say, "What's that brown stuff on your cheeks?" After thinking a moment, the neighbor would realize that a bear was meant — because black bears have brown markings around the nose and mouth. Or the visitor might ask, "How come you walk around like this?" while imitating a bear's pigeon-toed walk.

The guesser would not actually speak the word "bear." He would simply get ready to go hunting. If the bear overheard its name, it would be warned, and that could make the hunting expedition all the more dangerous.

## *Dream guessing*

The Onondaga of New York State use riddles to express
the idea that members of the community stand willing to
help each other in time of need. This is an ancient and
very serious custom that has continued into the twentieth
century.

During the ceremony of midwinter, people who have
had troubling dreams — dreams that indicate a need or a
strong desire — announce the fact by putting their dream
into the form of a riddle. Everyone struggles to come up
with a guess. When at last the correct answer is heard,
there is a general cry of relief, "*Wa-o-wa-o-waaaa!*," and a
singer acting on behalf of the dreamer performs a song of
thanks. To conclude the business, the correct guesser then
promises to give the dreamer a gift of food or some small
present.

Not only the Onondaga, but other Iroquoian tribes,
particularly the Seneca, the Cayuga, and the ancient
Huron, have similar rituals, or did have at one time. The
Onondaga and Huron riddles in this book are dream-
guessing riddles.

## *"Those who live will understand it"*

In other parts of the world, particularly Africa, riddles are
sometimes given to young people as an initiation test to
see whether they are ready for adulthood. Although no
rituals of this kind have been reported in the Americas, it
is possible that the Maya of Yucatan used to have riddle
tests to determine whether chiefs were fit for office.

According to the Book of Chilam Balam of Chumayel, a Maya manuscript over a hundred and fifty years old, the chiefs had to guess riddles at the end of each twenty-year period. The Native writer who copied the riddles explained the situation in explicit terms:

"Those who die are those who do not understand; those who live will understand it. The competitive test shall hang over the chiefs of the towns; it has been copied so that the severity may be known in which the reign is to end. . . . They shall be hung by the neck; the tips of their tongues shall be cut off; their eyes shall be torn out. On this day the end shall come."

It is not known, however, that such drastic punishment was ever meted out for unsuccessful riddle guessing. It may well be that the writer is stating a prophecy, a kind of wishful thinking directed against the Spanish rulers.

In any event, the quiz questions themselves are among the most colorful of American Indian riddles, and several are included in the present collection. All have the form "Son, tell me so-and-so," the answer to be given as "Father, it is such-and-such."


## Riddles and gambling

Another kind of riddling found in tribal cultures of Africa is the riddle contest, in which two teams match wits against each other. In the Americas, this kind of sport is rare. Only among the Comanche has it been reported, and only as a thing of the past.

In the twentieth century, the Comanche still remembered riddles (and a few will be found in this book). But the questions were no longer loaded with such suspense as in the early days.

Formerly the riddlers would choose sides, and members of the two teams would take turns stepping forward to ask a riddle or guess the answer. Sometimes the participants would place bets on the outcome.

Counters, like modern poker chips, might be used to keep score. Or, in some cases, the property being wagered would actually be laid out between the riddler and the guesser.

## *The riddle dance*

The Muinane, a tribe of the northwest Amazon region, used to hold nighttime riddling games that took the form of a dance. These were boisterous occasions, punctuated with shouts of laughter.

To begin, a warrior who had a reputation as a wit would enter the circle of players and chant a riddle. The others would then pick up the chant, repeating it as they danced around him. At a signal the dance would stop, and the riddler would rush up to one of the participants, holding a torch close to his face, repeating the question again.

If the guesser said, "*Jana* [I do not know]," he would have to follow behind the questioner and imitate his antics, which were supposed to give a clue to the riddle. Since all the riddles were animal riddles, there would soon be a long file of failed guessers hurrying to keep up with the leader, all mimicking the animal in question.

The first person to guess correctly became the next riddler, and the dance would begin again.

## *To pasture life*

Among the Quechua of Peru, young men and women between the ages of ten and twenty spend long hours herding sheep. If a boy happens to meet a girl out in the grasslands, while both are tending their flocks, he may flirt with her by throwing a few small stones. She may reply with an insult — or a riddle.

On special occasions, when they are free from work, boys and girls return in groups to the mountain pastures. Here, far from adult interference, the boys play music on their small guitars, called *chinlilis*, and both sexes tell riddles.

It is said that to be good in riddling is to be good in love, and in this atmosphere, relationships are formed that eventually lead to marriage. The sessions themselves are called *vida michiy*, which means "to pasture life." (There are five Peruvian riddles in this book, all from the Ayacucho region, where *vida michiy* is practiced.)

Courtship riddling has not been reported from other Indian cultures. But the practice is known in the Philippines, and it is similar to customs preserved in the old folklore of Europe and the Middle East, where young women or their parents used to ask riddles of men who came courting. It was thought that a man smart enough to answer correctly would make a worthy husband.

## *Riddles in stories*

Stories of the hero who has to solve a riddle in order to save his own life, or of the clever woman who solves riddles and marries the king, are well known in European folklore. In Native America, such tales are rare. Yet there are excellent examples from at least two tribes, the Kekchi of Belize and the Arapaho of Oklahoma.

The Kekchi tell of two little boys, Sun and Morning Star, who lost their parents and had to live with their cruel grandmother. While the boys were taking their naps, the old woman would entertain her gentleman friend, serving him all the meat she had in the house.

Before leaving, the man would smear a little grease on the sleeping children's lips. Then, when they woke up crying for food, the grandmother would insist that they had eaten already. To prove her point, she would tell them to lick their lips.

Outraged, the boys challenged the old woman to a riddle contest, the loser to pay with his or her life. (The Kekchi arrow riddle included in this book is the very riddle that stumped the grandmother, giving the boys their excuse to shoot her dead.)

Arapaho tales of boy heroes who match wits with the spirit of winter are another source of Indian riddles. In one of the stories, as the boy answers the spirit's questions, the spirit keeps shrinking until it is nothing but a pool of water — and spring has come. All the Arapaho riddles in the present collection are from that story of the hero Raw Gums and the winter spirit called White Owl.

Finally, at the end of this book there are two stories made up almost entirely of riddles. In the first, from the Pawnee, riddles make a man sick; but the answers cure him. The second story is a tiny trickster tale from the Pehuenche tribe of Chile in which the fox is outwitted by the clever thrush, who stores up all the fox's riddles in his memory, then reels off the answers in a single breath.

## The art of riddling

No doubt it helps to have a superhuman memory or to be as quick-witted as the legendary heroes of folklore. Yet ordinary human beings have ways of solving riddles, too.

The first thing to remember is that riddles often begin with what folklorists call "opening formulas." For example, Alaskan riddlers may start by saying "Riddle me" or "Wait!" In Peru, people say, "What is it? How many? What can it be?"

These expressions simply mean that a riddle is about to be asked. Probably the answer will have nothing to do with "waiting" or "how many."

The second point to remember — which has already been mentioned — is that a great many riddles seem to describe a person yet really mean a thing or an animal. Sometimes the opening formula deliberately throws the guesser off the track. If a riddle begins, "There's an old man . . ." or "There's a person . . . ," the guesser should be warned that the answer will *not* be a person.

Also, it helps to know that the subject matter of riddles tends to run in certain channels. It is surprising to discover that most Indian riddles — and riddles the world over — concern just four topics: plants, animals, tools, and parts of the human body. For Native America, a fifth important topic may be added: elements of nature (such as wind, water, sky, and earth). As an aid to the guesser, the riddles in this book have been arranged by category.

Most pages have been printed with two or more riddles at the top and the answers in smaller type at the bottom — so that you may cover the answers with your hand.

Of course, many people appreciate riddles as a form of poetry, without feeling they have to solve them.

For those who wish to test their wits, it may help to add one last word of encouragement. Although Native American riddlers typically insist that the only correct answer is the answer they themselves have in mind, there are times when more than one answer is acceptable. In any case, a guess that makes sense, whether "right" or not, deserves a well-earned *"haku."*

The Natural World

What is it that shines when the sun goes down?


What is that turns the day dark?


the moon
*Brazil: Cashinawa*


the night
*Brazil: Cashinawa*

Riddle me: I reach beyond the distant hills.


What is it that cuts off the night?


What is it that burns people when it gets up?


moonlight
*Alaska : Koyukon*


the dawn
*Brazil : Cashinawa*


the sun
*Brazil : Cashinawa*

There's a pepper seed in the water.


There's a star in the water.

it's a star
*Mexico : Chatino*


it's the eye of a fish
*Oklahoma : Comanche*

There are two people who look at each other.

What is it? A blue bowl filled with popcorn.

Every four weeks it becomes a baby. Who is it?

sky and earth
*Mexico:Amuzgo*

the sky with its stars
*Mexico:Aztec*

the moon
*Mexico:Amuzgo*

The old man is wrinkling his forehead.


What noise makes you feel small?


Threads of seven colors are stretched on
    the great prairie.


it's lightning
*Mexico : Chatino*


thunder
*Oklahoma : Comanche*


rainbow
*Peru : Quechua*

There's a person who's all over the earth.

A hand over the world.

the air
*Mexico:Amuzgo*

darkness
*Alaska:Ahtna*

Wait, there is someone coming to
    us, but it is quiet again.


You grab it, I grab it.


You hear it hum, it hits you,
    but you don't see it.

a gust of wind
*Alaska : Tanaina*


air
*Yucatan : Maya*


the wind
*Yucatan : Maya*

What is it that has a red head?


Wait, I see little brothers chasing
    each other into the air.


They disappear in the dark.


Big as a willow, light as a weed.


the fire
*Brazil : Cashinawa*


sparks going up from the fire
*Alaska : Tanaina*


sparks
*Alaska : Ahtna*


smoke
*Peru : Quechua*

What is it? A scarlet macaw leads the way,
    a raven brings up the rear.


What is it that for one day has its own way?

grass fire
*Mexico : Aztec*


prairie fire
*Oklahoma : Comanche*

There's a person who's noisy day and night.

Every day
every night
the old man in the ravine
is calling.

**the creek**
*Mexico:Amuzgo*

**it's the river**
*Mexico:Chatino*

Riddle me: it sounds like a lullaby being sung
  to children in the other world.


Wait, I see lots of pretty nests.

a fast-moving current
*Alaska: Koyukon*

whirlpools made by
a canoe paddle
*Alaska: Tanaina*

Riddle me: we have our heads in sheepskin caps.

Riddle me: like a herd of deer lying down.

tree stumps after
a snowfall
*Alaska : Koyukon*

bare spots in the snow
*Alaska : Koyukon*

Riddle me: water is tearing away at my sides.


Watch me dance.
I am heavy
but I can dance.
See the edge of my skirt
wave back and forth.
It is the waves of the sea
on my beach. [Who is this?]

an island
*Alaska : Koyukon*


an island, dancing
*Mexico : Seri*

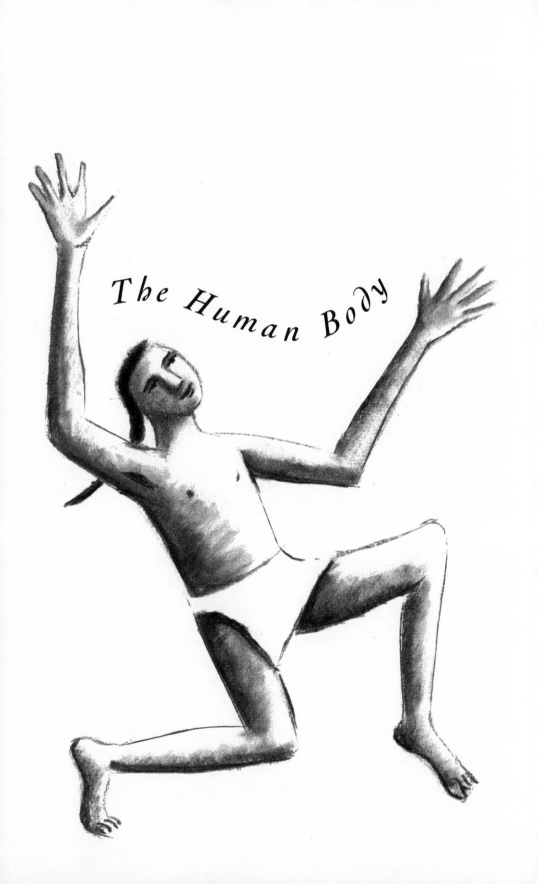

The Human Body

What is it? Has a wrinkled face,
    goes kicking along.


Wonder, wonder,
What can we be?
Me first,
You next.

your knee
*Mexico : Aztec*

two feet
*Paraguay : Guaraní*

Son, whom did you see on
the road? Did you see an
old man with his little boys?

Father, here is the old
man I saw on the road, also
the boys. They are with
me, they do not leave me:
they are the big toe
with the little toes.

*Yucatan:Maya*

Son, did you see the old woman
    carrying her stepchildren?


What are they? Ten flat stones
    that we carry with us.


Who is it? Little Fleshy Face
    with the bony neck.

Father, they are here. They
are with me so that I may
eat. They are the thumb
and the other fingers.
*Yucatan : Maya*


our fingernails
*Mexico : Aztec*


it's just your finger
*Mexico : Aztec*

When you're little, it's big.
When you're big, it's little.
What is it?


What has two paths?


Wonder, wonder,
What can they be?
The two young women who sit side by side
    without seeing each other.

your belly button
*Argentina : Quechua*

your nose
*Oklahoma : Arapaho*

your ears
*Paraguay : Guaraní*

The cave has a pig in it.


Thirty-two bulls peep out of a cave.


it's the tongue in your mouth
*Mexico: Chatino*


teeth
*Peru: Quechua*

Son, did you pass by a water gutter?


Son, what did you do with your
      companion who was coming
      close behind you?


What is it? How many? What can it be?
      A widow that can't be caught.


Father, it is here,
it is with me.
It is the furrow
down my back.
*Yucatan:Maya*


Here is my companion.
I have not left it.
It is my shadow.
*Yucatan:Maya*


shadow
*Peru:Quechua*

Son, have you seen the green
    water holes in the rock?
    There are two of them.
    A cross is raised between them.


Wait, I see two lakes together.

they are a man's eyes
*Yucatan : Maya*


they are a man's eyes
*Alaska : Tanaina*

Riddle me: I make something touch far away.


What is it? A little mirror in a house
    made of fir branches.


our eyesight
*Alaska:Koyukon*


the eye with its lashes
*Mexico:Aztec*

I am doing it, and you are doing it.
　　　Can you guess what it is?


What is there inside you like lightning?


breathing
*Yucatan : Maya*


meanness
*Oklahoma : Comanche*

What is it that travels by night?

What travels fast?

ghosts
*Brazil : Cashinawa*

your thoughts
*Oklahoma : Arapaho*

Which of your two hands is more
valuable than the other?

your left hand, because it
is harmless, pure, and holy

*Oklahoma:Arapaho*

Animals

What is it that taught us
to make houses?

the wasps
*Brazil: Cashinawa*

Wonder, wonder,
What can it be?
An upside-down house
    with fifty thousand owners.


There is a place where a little drum hangs.


There is a place where babies are crying hard.


a beehive
*Paraguay : Guaraní*


beehive
*Mexico : Amuzgo*


bees
*Mexico : Amuzgo*

What is it? A black stone with its head
    to the ground, listening to the
    sounds of the underworld.


What is it? It runs through the valleys,
    clapping its hands.


What is it? Skinny little red thing,
    has no trouble eating you up.


beetle
*Mexico : Aztec*


butterfly
*Mexico : Aztec*


ant
*Mexico : Aztec*

What lives in a black forest
and dies on a white stone?


Why does a dog have a curl in its tail?

the lice we catch in our
hair and crush on our
fingernail
*Mexico : Aztec*


so fleas can
loop the loop
*North Carolina : Cherokee*

What is it that has its young ones
    in hollow trees?


What is it that cries in the night?

the scarlet macaw
*Brazil:Cashinawa*

the owl
*Brazil:Cashinawa*

Wait, I see a rich man's daughter
  dancing in the sky.


Riddle me: little dots seen far
  away in the distance.


It is light, it does not speak.
  What is it?

the arctic tern
flying stationary
with its wings fluttering
*Alaska : Tanaina*


the return of
migratory birds
*Alaska : Koyukon*


a gull's feather
*Labrador : Inuit*

What is it that travels with its young
    ones clinging to its sides?


What is it that bosses people?


the capuchin monkey
*Brazil: Cashinawa*


the capuchin monkey
— oh, what a riddle!
*Brazil: Cashinawa*

What is it that eats raw meat?


Who is the girl with yellow paint
on her cheeks?


jaguar
*Brazil : Cashinawa*


raccoon
*Oklahoma : Comanche*

Who's the good-looking young person
  in the striped blanket?


Which animal is stronger than all the others?

skunk
*Oklahoma : Comanche*


skunk
*Oklahoma : Comanche*

Riddle me: it looks like soft white
clouds around the sky.


What is it? A scary old woman
nibbling under the earth.

the fat around a
reindeer's fourth stomach
*Alaska : Koyukon*


gopher
*Mexico : Aztec*

There's a place where a stone sits in the
    middle of the water.


Riddle me: it looks like a stand
    of spruce trees.


Riddle me: we come upstream
    in red canoes.


turtle
*Mexico:Amuzgo*


whale's whiskers
*Alaska:Koyukon*


salmon
*Alaska:Koyukon*

Wait, I see a little red spark moving on
        top of the water.


Riddle me: I drag my shovel along the trail.

the swimming beaver's teeth
    in the setting sun
        *Alaska : Tanaina*


beaver
*Alaska : Koyukon*

Where does the mouse go when the
cat catches it?

it goes inside the cat
*New York:Seneca*

Things
That
Grow

Who are they? Little old men bending over
        us throughout the world.


Son, go bring me the girl with the
        watery teeth. Her hair is twisted
        into a tuft. Fragrant shall be her
        odor when I remove her garments.

corn tassels
*Mexico : Aztec*

it is an ear of green
corn cooked in a pit
*Yucatan : Maya*

What is it? A little white head with
    green plumes on top.


What wears a tight blouse?


**an onion**
*Mexico:Aztec*


**a tomato**
*Mexico:Aztec*

Wonder, wonder
What are these two?
One hugs its mother,
One kisses its daughter.

the orange and
the orange tree
*Paraguay : Guaraní*

Who is the person with teeth in his stomach?


What I desire and what I seek has a
   lake inside itself.

squash
*Mexico:Amuzgo*


it is this: a pumpkin
*Ontario:Huron*

Riddle me: I keep myself comfortable,
    wrapped in rich, soft furs.


Wonder, wonder,
What can I be?
I stick with you
    and we go together.

seeds of
the wild rose
*Alaska : Koyukon*


a thistle
*Paraguay : Guaraní*

Riddle me: we turn down our faces,
    gasping for breath.


Riddle me: we don't want to choke on smoke,
    so we're hiding our faces.

spruce cones
*Alaska:Koyukon*

a clump of spruce
cones curled under
*Alaska:Koyukon*

Has little shoes of earth.
    Whistles night and day.


Riddle me: I act as a broom,
    sweeping the place around me.

 

**grass**
*Peru : Quechua*


grass tops, when the wind
blows over the snow
*Alaska : Koyukon*

Things
Made
to Be
Used

Wonder, wonder,
What can it be?
Born in the woods,
　　　it lives on the river.

a canoe
*Paraguay: Guaraní*

Wonder, wonder,
What can it be?
Bald in the middle with hairy sides.


What goes all around the house
　　　and never comes in?

a path
*Paraguay : Guaraní*


path
*North Carolina : Cherokee*

What is it that has two heads?


At night it's full, in the day it's hungry.


a hammock
*Brazil: Cashinawa*


a hammock
*Yucatan: Maya*

What says [to its partner],
    "You jump, I jump"?


What is it that says to itself,
    "You go this way, I'll go that way,
    and we'll meet on the other side"?


What is it? Goes into the forest with
    its tongue hanging.


a drumstick
*Mexico:Aztec*


a loincloth
*Mexico:Aztec*


an ax
*Mexico:Aztec*

What do we live in?

There's a person who's very crybabyish.

a house
*Brazil: Cashinawa*

the door — it
always squeaks
*Mexico: Amuzgo*

What is it that never gets tired of
motioning people to come over?

Who are the ones that always stand
straight and pay attention?

the earflaps
of the tepee
*Oklahoma : Arapaho*

tepee stakes
*Oklahoma : Arapaho*

What is it? It's round, it sits on
    the stones, it sings.


It's grumbling. Beyond the mountain,
    smoke is rising: it chases away
    the reindeer. What is it?

the cooking pot
*Mexico : Aztec*


a boiling kettle —
children, take care!
*Labrador : Inuit*

Wonder, wonder,
Who can she be?
The dark lady on her golden chair.

a pot on the fire

*Paraguay: Guaraní*

Wonder, wonder,
What are these three?
A plump mother,
A bearded father,
A little boy coming and going.

stove, broom, and shovel
*Paraguay: Guaraní*

It has holes, yet it catches.
　　What is it?


Wonder, wonder,
What can it be?
Put your hand in its eyes
　　and it starts to eat.

the net of a
lacrosse stick
*New York : Onondaga*


scissors
*Paraguay : Guaraní*

What is it, what is it?
Goes to water but not to drink,
Goes out to pasture but not to eat,
Lies down, but it never sleeps.


Wonder, wonder,
What can it be?
It walks with its tongue.


cowbell
*Argentina : Quechua*


a plow
*Paraguay : Guaraní*

What goes into the air, travels along,
and drops down again?

Riddle me: it glides along, tapping its
forehead against the air.

an arrow
*Belize : Kekchi*

an arrowhead
*Alaska : Koyukon*

I am alone.
If we were married,
We would go out early.
We would kill a deer.

the arrow's love
song to the bow
*Mexico : Seri*

Story of Speak-Riddles and Wise-Spirit

Speak-Riddles crossed to the other side of the village and said to Wise-Spirit, "I want to give you riddles, because I understand you know how to solve them."

"All right," said Wise-Spirit. "Let me hear them."

Then Speak-Riddles told them:

As you saw me coming toward you, you thought there were two of us.

Then you saw people coming toward the village, grasping their hair, as though crying.

Then close to the village there was something flying.

A red bird was killed.

There must have been trees uprooted — the roots are turned up.

As I looked at the sides of the hills, I saw as if many black lariat ropes.

Near the village I heard a whistling.

As I came near one lodge, I saw a grandmother bending over, and she seemed to have many skulls beside her.

When Wise-Spirit had heard the riddles,
he went home. But instead of figuring them out,
he began to have a headache and got sick. People thought he was dying.

"I want Speak-Riddles to tell me the answers before I die," he said. "Then I can die happy."

Speak-Riddles came to him and said:

*As you saw me coming toward you, you thought
there were two of us.* I mean that you saw two of
us — myself and my shadow.

*Then you saw people coming toward the village,
grasping their hair, as though crying.* I mean there
were men carrying meat on their backs: they
hold the load close to their ears, as if grasping
their hair, and the sweat rolls down their
cheeks as if they are crying.

*Then close to the village there was something
flying.* I mean a stream — and the rippling of the
water that sounded like a bird in flight.

*A red bird was killed.* I mean that as I
crossed the stream I saw a plum tree and plums
on the ground as if a red bird had been killed
there.

*There must have been trees uprooted — the roots
are turned up.* I mean there were many dead buffalo on the prairie, and as their carcasses dried,
their bones stuck up like tree roots.

*As I looked at the sides of the hills, I saw as if many black lariat ropes.* I mean there were many rows of buffalo in single file on the hills.

*Near the village I heard a whistling.* I mean there were women scraping buffalo hides, making a whistling sound as they whetted the points of their knives.

*As I came near one lodge, I saw a grandmother bending over, and she seemed to have many skulls beside her.* I mean I saw an old woman scraping tallow from bones, so that balls of tallow lay all around her in the shape of skulls.

As Speak-Riddles mentioned each thing, Wise-Spirit thanked him and got better each time. Finally Wise-Spirit said, "My grandfather, I thank you for these riddles. You are the first one to give me riddles I could not make out. I am now a well man. Stay with me, for I want to get strong; then you shall go home." And Speak-Riddles did.

*Oklahoma : Pawnee*

Story of the Fox
and the
Thrush

"Let's play a game, friend thrush," said the fox.

"Yo," said the thrush, "what game shall we play?" said the thrush.

"I'll tell you riddles, you'll answer them all," said the fox.

"Yo," said the thrush.

Then the fox told riddles:

It goes hopping along the trail, what is it?
It lies across the trail, what is it?

It runs with a clatter of hooves, what is it?
It runs at a trot, what is it?

I scratch in the earth, who am I?
I burrow into the earth, who am I?
I burrow into the oak, who am I?

It's over your head and it's red, what is it?
It's over your head and it's round,
    what is it?

"Now answer them all," said the fox to the thrush.

Toad.
Snake.

Cow.
Horse.

Pig.
Mouse.
Tree fungus.

Cherry.
Apple.

*Chile : Pehuenche*

# Who the Riddlers Are

New sources of Indian riddles continued to be discovered into the 1980s. Probably more will come to light. At present, it seems that at least thirty tribes or cultures have some kind of riddling tradition. It also appears that these groups are concentrated in three main regions:

> central Alaska (Ahtna, Koyukon, Kutchin, Tanaina, Tanana)
>
> southern Mexico (Amuzgo, Aztec, Chatino, Kekchi, Lacandon, Maya, Popoluca, Tzotzil)
>
> western South America (Aymara, Cashinawa, Chipaya, Mapuche, Muinane, Pehuenche, Quechua, Sirionó)

In addition, at least three tribes from the southern Great Plains can be included (Arapaho, Comanche, and Pawnee), at least three from the region of Lake Ontario (Huron, Onondaga, and Seneca) — and a few that lie outside the areas that have been mentioned.

The following list of tribes serves as a riddle index, keyed to the page numbers in this book.

AHTNA (OTT-nuh). An Athapaskan tribe of east central Alaska. Riddles on pp. 20 and 22. Source: James Kari in Dauenhauer, *Riddle and Poetry Handbook*.

AMUZGO (uh-MOOSE-go). A group of about a dozen communities clustered near the southern border of Oaxaca and Guerrero states, Mexico. Riddles on pp. 18, 20, 24, 46, 55, 64, and 75. Source: Scott.

ARAPAHO (uh-RAP-uh-ho). A Plains tribe of two divisions: the Southern Arapaho, who have settled in Oklahoma, and the Northern Arapaho, now on reservation lands in central Wyoming. Riddles (all from the Southern Arapaho) on pp. 34, 40, 41, and 76. Source: G. Dorsey and Kroeber.

ARAUCANIAN. See MAPUCHE and PEHUENCHE.

AYMARA (eye-muh-RAH). A people of Bolivia and adjacent Peru, numbering about one million speakers. Three riddles are given by Scott.

AZTEC. The native people of Mexico City, who controlled an empire stretching from the Gulf of Mexico to the Pacific Coast — until they were conquered by the Spanish in 1521. Riddles on pp. 18, 23, 31, 33, 38, 47, 48, 54, 61, 62, 74, and 77. Translated from the Aztec in Sahagún.

CASHINAWA (kah-shee-nah-WAH). A forest tribe of western Brazil and eastern Peru. Riddles on pp. 15, 16, 22, 40, 45, 49, 51, 52, 73, and 75. Translated from the Cashinawa and Portuguese texts in Abreu.

CHATINO (chuh-TEE-no). A tribe of about 20,000 persons in the highlands of southeastern Oaxaca State, Mexico. Riddles on pp. 17, 19, 24, and 35. Source: Upson.

CHEROKEE. A people of the southeastern United States, now divided between western North Carolina and eastern Oklahoma. But the Cherokee riddles given in this book (pp. 48 and 72) are from a group in eastern North Carolina, sometimes calling themselves Cherokee, more commonly called Croatan or Lumbee. Source: Parsons, "Folk-Lore of the Cherokee of Robeson County, North Carolina."

CHIPAYA (chuh-PIE-uh). A small tribe of southwestern Bolivia. Three riddles are given by Scott.

COMANCHE (kuh-MAN-chee). A once wide-ranging Plains tribe, now settled in Oklahoma. Riddles on pp. 17, 19, 23, 39, 52, and 53. Source: McAllester.

GUARANÍ (gwah-ruh-NEE). A people of Paraguay and northern Argentina. Riddles on pp. 31, 34, 46, 63, 65, 71, 72,
78, 79, 80, and 81. Translated from the Spanish in
Lehmann-Nitsche, *Adivinanzas*. Other Guaraní riddles are
in Lehmann-Nitsche, *Textos*.

HURON. An Iroquoian tribe, formerly in southern Ontario.
Riddle on p. 64. Source: Blau.

INUIT (IN-yoo-it). The preferred Native name for the Eskimo,
especially the Eskimo of Canada and Greenland. The riddles on pp. 50 and 77 are from the Inuit of Labrador.
Souce: Boas.

IROQUOIAN. See HURON, ONONDAGA, and SENECA.

KEKCHI (KEK-chee). A Mayan tribe of Belize and eastern
Guatemala. Riddle on p. 82. Source: Thompson.

KOYUKON (kah-yoo-KON or koy-yoo-KON). An Athapaskan tribe of central Alaska. Riddles on pp. 16, 26, 27, 50,
55 (3d), 56, 65, 66 (2d), 67, and 82 are from Jetté; on pp.
25, 38, 54, 55 (2d), and 66 (1st), from Chief Henry. Another source of Koyukon riddles: Nelson.

KUTCHIN (koo-CHIN). Also called Gwich'in. An Athapaskan
tribe of Alaska and northwestern Canada. Hunters' riddles
are reported in Mishler.

LACANDON (lah-kun-DOHN). A small Mayan tribe of southeastern Mexico. One riddle is given by Scott.

MAPUCHE (muh-POO-chay). An Araucanian tribe of central
Chile. Unusual riddles (in which the riddler gives the first
syllable of a word and asks the guesser to complete it) are
in Guevara. Conventional riddles are in Aguilera et al.

MAYA. As used in this book, the term refers only to the Yucatec,
the Maya of Yucatan. (In a broader sense, it refers to any

of the Mayan-speaking tribes of Mexico and western Central America, including the KEKCHI, LACANDON, and TZOTZIL.) Riddles on pp. 21 and 73 are from Burns; on p. 39, from Andrade; on pp. 32, 33, 36, 37, and 61, from Roys. Other sources of Maya riddles: M. Redfield, R. Redfield and Villa Rojas, Solís Alcalá, Toor.

MICMAC. A tribe of eastern Canada. Riddles borrowed from Euro-Americans are in Parsons, "Micmac Folklore."

MUINANE (mwee-nah-NAY). A tribe of the northwest Amazon region (south bank of the Caquetá River in southern Colombia), reported in the early twentieth century. Riddle dance described by Whiffen.

OMAHA. A tribe of eastern Nebraska. Three riddles borrowed from a non-Indian source are given by J. O. Dorsey, discussed by Dundes.

ONONDAGA. An Iroquoian tribe of central New York. Riddle on p. 80. Source: Blau.

PAWNEE. A tribe of the southern Great Plains, with survivors in Oklahoma. Riddles on pp. 87–89. Source: G. Dorsey.

PEHUENCHE (puh-WEN-chay). Name given to one or more Araucanian tribes of the southern Andes, usually meaning Araucanians on the Argentine side of the border — but used by Lenz to mean Chileans. Riddles on pp. 93–94. Translated from the Spanish in Lenz.

PENOBSCOT. A Maine tribe. The activities of the village "riddle-men" are discussed by Speck.

POPOLUCA. A Mexican tribe in the region where Veracruz, Puebla, and Oaxaca states come together. The existence of Popoluca riddles is reported by Scott.

QUECHUA (KETCH-wuh). The language of the ancient Incas, spoken today by about 8 million people in the central Andes from Ecuador to Argentina. Riddles from Ayacucho Department, Peru, on p. 36 (source: Isbell and Roncalla) and on pp. 19, 22, 35 and 67 (translated from the Spanish in Lara); from Santiago del Estero Province, Argentina, on pp. 34 and 81 (translated from the Spanish in Lehmann-Nitsche, *Adivinanzas*). Other Quechua riddles are in Lehmann-Nitsche, *Textos;* and in sources listed by Lara.

SENECA. An Iroquoian tribe of western New York. Riddle on p. 57. Source: Preston.

SERI (SAY-ree). A small desert tribe of Sonora State, northwestern Mexico. Riddle-like songs on pp. 27 and 83 are from Coolidge and Coolidge.

SIRIONÓ (seer-ee-o-NO). A small tribe of northeastern Bolivia. Riddle on p. 4. Source: Scott.

TANAINA (tuh-NIGH-nuh). An Athapaskan tribe of south central Alaska. Riddles on pp. 21, 22, 25, 37, 50, and 56. Source: Kari.

TANANA (TAN-uh-naw). An Athapaskan tribe of east central Alaska. Several riddles are given by Guédon. Mishler reports a further collection, as yet unpublished.

TZOTZIL (tsoht-SEEL). A Mayan group of Chiapas State, Mexico. Two riddles are given by Gossen.

# Sources

(The abbreviation JAF stands for *Journal of American Folklore.*)

Abreu, J. Capistrano de. *Rã-txa hu-ni-ku-ī: a lingua dos caxinauás.* Rio de Janeiro: Typographia Leuzinger, 1914. Riddles on pp. 520–23.

Aguilera Milla, P., et al. *Pu mapuche tani kimün.* Temuco, Chile: Universidad de la Frontera / Instituto Lingüístico de Verano, 1984.

Andrade Manuel J. "Yucatec Maya Stories." Microfilm Collection of Manuscripts on Cultural Anthropology, no. 262. Regenstein Library, University of Chicago, 1977. Riddles on folio 1648.

Blau, Harold. "Dream Guessing: A Comparative Analysis," *Ethnohistory* 10 (1963): 233–49.

Boas, Franz. "Two Eskimo Riddles from Labrador," JAF 39 (1926): 486.

Book of Chilam Balam of Mani. *See* Solís Alcalá.

Burns, Allan F. *An Epoch of Miracles: Oral Literature of the Yucatec Maya.* Austin: University of Texas Press, 1983. Riddles on pp. 228–31.

Chief Henry. *K'ooltsaah ts'in': Koyukon Riddles.* Transcribed and translated by Eliza Jones. Fairbanks: Alaska Native Language Center, 1976. This is a packet of 28 flash cards in the Koyukon language, with 4 additional cards giving English translations and comments by Chief Henry.

Coolidge, Dane, and Mary R. Coolidge. *The Last of the Seris.* Glorieta, New Mexico: Rio Grande Press. Originally published 1939.

Dauenhauer, Richard. "Koyukon Riddle-Poems," *Alcheringa,*

n.s., vol. 3, no. 1, pp. 85–90. 1977. Literary reworkings of 44 riddles from the collection of Jetté (see below).

———. *Koyukon Riddles*. Anchorage: Alaska Bilingual Education Center / Alaska Native Education Board, 1975. A 32-page booklet; riddles adapted from Jetté (see 102).

———. *Riddle and Poetry Handbook*. [Anchorage:] Alaska Native Education Board, 1976. This important 110-page essay, anthology, and workbook, designed for classroom use, inspired a riddle revival in Alaska during the late 1970s. Now rare. Copy in the possession of Richard Dauenhauer, Sealaska Heritage Foundation, Juneau.

Dorsey, George A. *Traditions of the Skidi Pawnee*. Memoirs of the American Folklore Society, vol. 8. Boston, 1904. Riddles on pp. 300–301.

———, and Alfred L. Kroeber. *Traditions of the Arapaho*. Field Columbian Museum, Anthropological Series, vol. 5. Chicago, 1903. Riddles on pp. 231–36, 304–9.

Dorsey, J. Owen. "Omaha Sociology," *Third Annual Report of the Bureau of [American] Ethnology, 1881–1882*. Smithsonian, 1884. Riddles on p. 334 — but see Dundes, below.

Dundes, Alan. "North American Indian Folklore Studies," *Journal de la Société des Américanistes*, 56 (1967): 53–79. See p. 57 for non-Indian source of Omaha riddles published by J.O. Dorsey.

Gossen, Gary. *Chamulas in the World of the Sun*. Cambridge: Harvard University Press, 1974. Riddles on pp. 115–20.

Guédon, Marie-Françoise. *People of Tetlin, Why Are You Singing?* Mercury Series, 9. Ottawa: National Museums of Canada, Ethnology Division, 1974. Riddles on p. 201.

Guevara, Tomás. *Folklore araucano*. Santiago, Chile: Imprenta Cervantes, 1911. Riddles on pp. 157–58.

Henry. *See* Chief Henry.

Isbell, Billie Jean, and Fredy Amilcar Roncalla Fernandez. "The Ontogenesis of Metaphor: Riddle Games among Quechua Speakers . . . ," *Journal of Latin American Lore* 3 (1977): 19–49.

Jetté, Jules. "Riddles of the Ten'a Indians," *Anthropos* 8 (1913): 181–201, 630–51.

Jones, Eliza. *See* Chief Henry.

Kari, James, ed. *K'ich'ighi: Dena'ina Riddles*. Collected by Albert Wassalie, Sr. Anchorage: University of Alaska, National Bilingual Materials Development Center (Rural Education), [1981]. Distributed by Mariswood Educational Resources, Aniak, Alaska.

Lara Irala, Edilberto. *Adivinanzas quechuas: Contribución al estudio de la literatura oral*. San Cristóbal de Huamanga, Peru: Ediciones Investigación Universitaria, 1981. Five hundred Quechua riddles with a bibliography of further sources.

Lehmann-Nitsche, Robert. *Adivinanzas rioplatenses*. Folklore Argentino, 1. Buenos Aires: Universidad de La Plata, 1911.

———. *Textos eróticos del Rio de la Plata*. Buenos Aires: Librería Clásica, 1981.

Lenz, Rodolf. "Estudios araucanos, VI," *Anales de la Universidad de Chile* 94 (1896): 95–120. Riddles on pp. 112–14.

McAllester, David P. "Riddles and Other Verbal Play Among the Comanches," JAF 77 (1964): 251–57.

Mishler, Craig. "Telling About Bear: A Northern Athapaskan Men's Riddle Tradition," JAF 97 (1984): 61–68.

Nelson, Richard K. *Make Prayers to the Raven: A Koyukon View of the Northern Forest*. Chicago: University of Chicago Press, 1983.

Parsons, Elsie Clews. "Folk-Lore of the Cherokee of Robeson County, North Carolina," JAF 32 (1919): 384–94.

———. "Micmac Folklore," JAF 38 (1925): 55–133.

——— *Peguche*. Chicago: University of Chicago Press, 1945. For Spanish riddles obtained from Quechua informants see pp. 126–127.

Preston, W. D. "Six Seneca Jokes," JAF 62 (1949): 426–27.

Redfield, Margaret Park. "The Folk Literature of a Yucatecan Town," *Contributions to American Archaeology*, no. 13, pp. 1–50. Carnegie Institution of Washington, 1935. Riddles on pp. 49–50.

Redfield, Robert, and Alonso Villa R[ojas]. *Chan Kom: A Maya Village*. Carnegie Institution of Washington, 1934. Riddles on pp. 329–30.

Roys, Ralph L. *The Book of Chilam Balam of Chumayel*. Norman: University of Oklahoma Press, 1967. Riddles on pp. 88–98, 103, 125–31. A newer translation, by Munro S. Edmonson, is published as *Heaven Born Merida and Its Destiny* (Austin: University of Texas Press, 1986).

Sahagún, Bernardino de. *Códice florentino*. 3 vols. Mexico: Secretaría de Gobernación, 1979. Riddles in vol. 2, libro 6, folios 197v–199v. An English-Aztec edition of libro 6 of the *Códice florentino*, prepared by Arthur J. O. Anderson and Charles Dibble, is published as *Florentine Codex*, Book 6 (Salt Lake City: University of Utah Press, 1969).

Scott, Charles T. "New Evidence of American Indian Riddles," JAF 76 (1963): 236–44.

Solís Alcalá, Ermilio, ed. *Códice Pérez* [the Book of Chilam Balam of Mani]. Merida: Liga de Acción Social, 1949. Riddles on p. 73.

Speck, Frank G. *Penobscot Man*. Philadelphia: University of Pennsylvania Press, 1940. Riddling tradition on p. 269.

Taylor, Archer. "American Indian Riddles," JAF 57 (1944): 1–15. The first serious discussion suggesting that riddles might be native to the Americas.

Thompson, J. Eric S. *Ethnology of the Mayas of Southern and Central British Honduras*. Field Museum of Natural History, Anthropological Series, vol. 17, no. 2. Chicago, 1930. Riddles on p. 123.

Toor, Frances. *A Treasury of Mexican Folkways*. New York: Crown, 1947. Maya riddles on p. 540.

Upson, Jessamine. "Some Chatino Riddles Analyzed," *International Journal of American Linguistics* 22 (1956): 113–16.

Whiffen, Thomas. *The North-west Amazons*. New York: Duffield, 1915. Riddle dance on pp. 201–2.